CUMBRIA LIBRARIES

3 8003 04798 5379

KT-151-634

Get Out of My Bath!

nosy crow

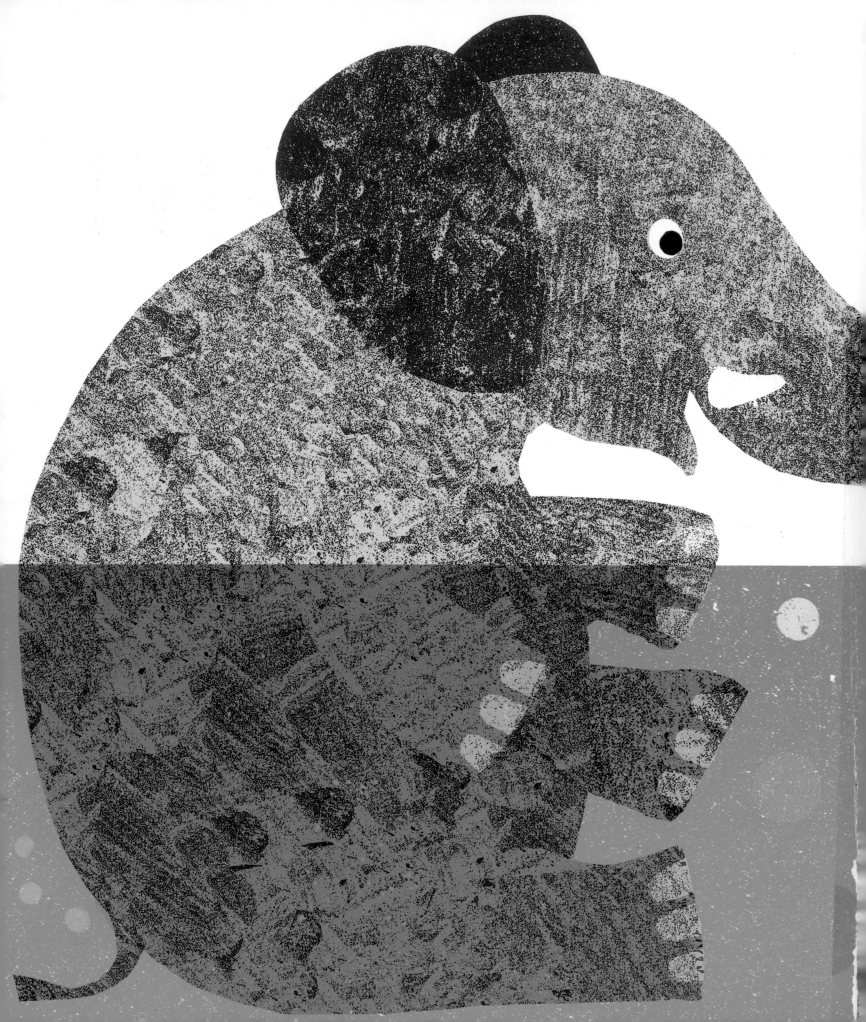

It's Ellie's bathtime.

Hello Ellie!

Ellie **loves** waves.
Can you help her make some?
Gently shake the book from
side to side and see what happens
when you turn the page . . .

Well done!

Look at those waves!
Ellie wants to play some more.
Now tilt the book to the left
and see what happens . . .

Hooray!

This is **fun!**
Now tilt the book to the right!

But what's this?

There's a **crocodile** in Ellie's bath!
And he's taken Ellie's rubber duck.
Ellie does **not** look happy. Can you shout,

"Get out, Crocodile!"

Can you shout louder?

Oh dear!

That didn't work.
Crocodile is
still there!

And now Flamingo is in the bath, too!

And look . . .

Tiger has just
jumped in with a
great big . . .

Splash!

This bath is **very** crowded.
Surely no one else can fit in.

Eeek! **It's a mouse!** Now there really are too many animals in this bath. Let's try to shake them out. Start shaking!

Can you shake harder?

That hasn't helped at all! And it looks like
Ellie's had **enough**. She shouts,

"Get out of my bath!"

Can **you** shout too? But what is Ellie up to?
She's sucking up **all** the water with
her long trunk until . . .

...all of the
water has gone.

BBRRR!

The animals are shivering.
Can you shiver, too?
"Let's go!" they say,
and they all disappear.

And when Ellie is sure that the animals have **really** left . . .

she **squirts** all the water back into her bath!

Aaaahh!

Now there's **lots** of room
in Ellie's bath again.
Clever Ellie!

And thank you for helping.

Maybe it's time for
your bath now?

To Silke
– B.T.

First
published in 2015
by Nosy Crow Ltd
The Crow's Nest,
10a Lant Street
London SE1 1QR
www.nosycrow.com
This edition published 2016
ISBN 978 0 85763 446 7 (PB)
Nosy Crow and associated logos
are trademarks and/or
registered trademarks of
Nosy Crow Ltd.
Text and illustration © Britta Teckentrup 2015
The right of Britta Teckentrup to be identified
as the author and illustrator of
this work has been asserted.
All rights reserved

This book is
sold subject to
the condition that
it shall not, by way
of trade or otherwise,
be lent, hired out or
otherwise circulated in any
form of binding or cover other
than that in which it is published.
No part of this publication may be
reproduced, stored in a retrieval system,
or transmitted in any form or by any means
(electronic, mechanical, photocopying,
recording or otherwise)
without the prior written permission of
Nosy Crow Ltd.
A CIP catalogue record for this book is available
from the British Library.

Printed in China

Papers used by Nosy Crow are made from
wood grown in sustainable forests.
1 3 5 7 9 8 6 4 2 (PB)